LOCKDOWN

Other Books by Madeleine Linda Isaac

Me: A Collection of Children's Poetry
Animal Adventure

LOCKDOWN

A Collection of West
Indian Short Stories

Madeleine Linda Isaac

Library of Congress Control Number:		2020925376
ISBN:	Hardcover	978-1-6641-4859-8
	Softcover	978-1-6641-4858-1
	eBook	978-1-6641-4905-2

Print information available on the last page.

Rev. date: 12/17/2020

To order additional copies of this book, contact:
Xlibris
844-714-8691
www.Xlibris.com
Orders@Xlibris.com
822727

CONTENTS

The Coconut Vendor...1

Prayers 5

Insane Fire...10

The Friendship..16

The Scarlet Ibis 19

The Chinese Mango 23

Corn Soup Queen 27

The Mystery of the Mangrove 30

Carnival Queen...35

Falling Apart...38

The Scent of the Wild Orchid 43

Winning Smile... 46

To my mother, Mona Garib

I wish to express sincere gratitude to Richard Brown for his encouragement to complete the task and advice about appropriateness and relevance of various elements in the book.

The Coconut Vendor

The green and yellow nuts piled high on his bicycle slid from side to side as he slowly rode up the dirt track. I wondered why everybody called him Boy when his arse was as old as the Arima Dial according to my mother. "Look, the old scamp coming," my mother said in a jovial tone. "He still have some money for meh from since the last time he buy coconut from meh, but I waiting for he tail," she continued. I also wondered why nobody ever robbed Boy when he was always advertising his thick wad of old crumpled up dollar bills. It did not matter if a customer needed change or not, he still pulled out his bank. No one ever attempted to rob him, maybe because of the sharp blade that he always carried around and was so versed at using. It was a sight to see Boy cut open a coconut. He did it with an accelerated grace that would mesmerize anyone and make him or her want to be a coconut vendor. Not so much for the thick wad of dollars but for the skill of being able to use the sharp blade and carve the nut however one desired, like a potter molding clay. After cutting the nuts, he would rub the sharp side of the blade on the ground; it made a bloodcurdling sound. Maybe the sharp blade was the deterrent after all.

I also wondered about his family, if he had a wife or children, and how he came to live in our village. Whenever I asked my mother she would angrily respond, "Mind yuh own business, yuh too dam fast for a child. Keep out big people business." I have never heard anyone ever talking about Boy or his family. He lived alone in a tiny wooden hut at the edge of the cane field. His yard was always well kept. Fruit trees of every kind bordered the outer perimeter and vegetables the inner perimeter. The trees and shrubs looked green, healthy, and were always laden with fruits and vegetables as if nothing was ever harvested. It was as if he had the Midas touch, everything he did was done with such harmony, neatness, and grace.

Boy was a calm and friendly person, always getting into a conversation with his customers. He used every opportunity to fill them in on the political happenings as he attended every political meeting of all the political parties. He was an optimist and believed that things would get better one day, and so he conveyed this hope to all who would listen. His toothless smile was a definite winner. I loved Boy. I could stand up for hours and watch him cut coconut and listen to him talk politics. When he spoke, he took time to pronounce every syllable and stress even when there was no need to do so. He had an unusual accent that I could not figure out. It sounded like a cocktail of American, British, and Indian. It was as if he knew everything about everything. He always wore a fedora hat that he tilted slightly to the left side. The first three buttons of his shirt were undone and tucked neatly into his trousers with a tight belt. The legs of his trousers were rolled up to his knees and his bare feet spread out on the unpaved road. He had a nice tan complexion from overexposure to the sun. Never mind he was lean in build, he managed his overloaded bicycle and his cutlass with much grace.

The girls in the village loved to stand up and watch Boy slice the leathery husks off, leaving a small hole at the top of the nut. When he knew they were looking at him he did it faster and with more charm. All the young boys in the village wanted to be a coconut vendor. My two younger brothers could not wait to grow old enough to be able to handle a cutlass. All the games they played entailed some mimicry of Boy, his bicycle, his cutlass, and wad of money.

Boy was always a happy soul; however, when election was near he would be in his glee. These days he was extra happy as the general election was a few days away. He did not miss the opportunity to remind everyone he came into contact with that it was their civic duty to vote for who they saw fit to govern this beautiful land. Boy worked from Sunday to Sunday from morning to night. Whenever Boy came to our house to buy coconut from my mother, he would cut one for me. "Pick one you like, child," he would say. I would always choose the big yellow nuts as they had more jelly than the green nuts. The water tasted bland in my mouth, so with three gulps I would drink it out. However, I was always eager for Boy to cut open the yellow nut and reveal the thick white jelly. I loved to see him create a spoon from the husk of the yellow nut for me to spoon out the delight. It tasted magical in my mouth and felt heavenly as it slid down my throat. I could not get enough of this soft white comfort, so I looked forward to him coming to buy coconut from my mother. Strangely, I never saw Boy drinking coconut juice or eating the jelly.

On my way from school that humid Thursday afternoon, I stopped to have one of my usual conversations with Boy. I was always amazed by his wealth of political knowledge. Few people in our village showed any interest in politics but not me, I wanted to know it the voices of Renzi and Butler made any impact on the leaders, if there were any benefits for my father and the other sugarcane workers, if the prices of foodstuff will increase. Who better to chat with than the local politician Boy? "Good evening, Uncle Boy. So what you think about the increase that the workers asking for? Yuh think they will get it?" I curiously questioned.

"Well, my child, to tell you the truth, I most solemnly do believe they will. Let me explain why I share this view. I think that the government will give in to their demand because they would not want uproar and also because they want the votes of the people. That is why you must encourage your father and mother to go out and vote on Monday," he instructed with much care in pronunciation and enunciations. The whole time we were conversing he was busy shining his bicycle and his cutlass even though both cutlass and bicycle looked fine to me. The conversation was exhilarating and went on for about twenty minutes. A feeling of pride filled me to the brim as I walked away feeling that I knew more than anybody else in my house. I felt like Matthew, like I had just received a degree. Matthew was the only person in our village to earn a bachelor of arts degree in something and had recently returned from England.

Sometime late that evening, during dinner I tried to engage my father in a conversation on politics but he would have none of it. "Son, you sounding just like Boy. Just relax yourself and eat your dinner. You need to spend some time with Matthew," was his response. As I was biting into my hot *sada roti* and *dasheen bhaji* I heard a commotion outside. My father went outside to investigate. We could hear Santana's voice in a low tone saying something about Boy. As I strained my ear to hear, all I heard was that the money was missing and who could do something like this. After sometime my father came back inside and broke the news to us that Boy was missing. My world fell apart at that moment. I was in disbelief. Boy and I just had the best conversation ever. How could this happen? Who could do something like this? This must be a joke, I told myself. I was planning to spend election day with Boy as I had no school. A sadness that I had never experienced before filled my soul. I knew Boy better than anyone in the village did, and I knew that he would soon show up to claim his bicycle and sharp cutlass.

His old shiny bicycle, still overladen with coconuts and his cutlass, lay on the dry cracked earth by the Chinese shop but his thick wad of dollars could not be found anywhere. It was like he just vanished from the village. Even the atmosphere was different. The calmness that accompanied his life seemed to accompany his disappearance. No one knew anything, no one saw anything, and no one heard anything, not even the police. This was the strangest occurrence; the sleepy village was thrown into dismay. People gathered in every nook and cranny of the village discussing Boy's disappearance in hushed tones. Some of the men combed the entire village and surrounding villages, looking in every dirt track, footpath, garden, abandoned house, cow pen, and even latrine, but Boy was nowhere to be found. Ved, the butcher, and some of the hunters took their dogs and went into the bushes for two days searching, but there was no sign of Boy. Santana and his son-in-law Gunzo decided to dive down into the river to look for Boy but came up empty-handed. Every group was hoping that the other had better luck and that Boy was alright. Days passed and still no sign of the local politician. This sent the peaceful village into shock and mourning. How would we survive when election was only a day away? No political news, no smiles, no coconuts.

Prayers

"Two with slight, no sweet sauce, and some roasted pepper on the side," Johnny calmly said. He looked on intently as *bhowjee* placed the thin oily *bara* on the paper, dropped a spoonful of steaming spicy curry *channa*, some cucumber chutney, some *mudder in law*, and some pepper *choka*. Placed another *bara* on top and handed it to the man in front of him. Johnny automatically started to chew as the man bit into his greasy delight. He ate up his two slights, paid, then rubbed his stomach and said to the waiting crowd, "Ah boy, I now ready for meh wife food, ah wonder what she cook," and slowly walked off.

Johnny opened the rough pine door to revealed Tina and Franka laughing scandalously and adding corn dumpling to the pot of oil down on the open fire. Tina had peeled and sliced the yellow breadfruit earlier that day. Making oil down was always a big thing. The preparation had to be done from the morning. One had to get the right type of breadfruit—the yellow one, that is—and it had to be at the right stage of maturation where it was not too young and not too full. One also had to get a good sweet dry coconut, grate it, extract the milk, and add it to the pot to give the final touch to the oil down. In order to test if the coconut was right for the oil down, one had to put it close to the ear and shake it to hear if it had water inside. Only then would one decide if a pot of oil down was going to be dinner. Franka pushed the dried mango logs further into the fire to create more heat so as to speed up the process, as Johnny was no joker with his belly and this could be seen from his protruding stomach.

A short man with sharp eyes and a big mouth. Johnny's voice could be heard all the way from Ravine Sable junction. But he had a good heart and treated Franka well. He would always buy her a piece of cloth from

---

the Indian store for her birthday and Christmas so she could make a new dress to wear on these special occasions. He even allowed her to go to the village bazaar with Tina. Tina and Franka immediately became good friends since she married Johnny and moved to Ravine Sable. Franka was generally a quiet person; however, whenever she was around Tina she was a different person. She would laugh scandalously, speak loudly, and use brash words. Tina was Johnny's youngest sibling, feisty and independent—maybe because she was afforded the rare privilege of working outside of the home. She worked at Ramsingh's Fabric Shop in the heart of the small town. This made her the envy of all the young ladies in the village.

"Yuh ready for the match on Saturday, Pally?" questioned Lal. "Boy, I always ready. I just practicing meh chant," was Lal's confident response. Lal was short for Lalbeharry. He was a thick, muscular specimen. He looked like a cross between the Black Stalin and Theodore Roosevelt. The shade of his complexion knew no darker, and his hair was needle straight. A huge pudgy nose and two small bright eyes set on his black face with a thick full head of hair falling around his face gave him a queer look. He looked like an indentured laborer from Madras just jumped off the *Fatel Razack.*

He'd been the champion stick fighter for the past four consecutive years. He was eager to make it his fifth. He came from a long generation of great stick fighters; it was in his blood, as the villagers would say. The prize this year was very tempting. He wondered to himself, What I go do with all that money if I win? Stuepes, let me stop with this wishful thinking, yes. Pally, his old friend, came to see him that day. "A, a wah going on?" Lal continued. "Well, I come to see how the preparation coming for Saturday. Remember that is the dey big day. Ah have ah idea for yuh, how yuh could win the fight. Now yuh doh have to do it, is up to you. Yuh ever think about getting you *poui* mounted?" Pally softly and slowly said as if every word cost him money and energy.

"Wah, you crazy! Wah kind of talk is this I hearing from a man like you?" Lal blurted out.

Quickly came the response, "Well, I just saying that the stakes high and Johnny not taking his eyes off that prize. Yuh doh have to listen to me, just do what you please. Well anyway, I just come to tell you dat and ah gone dey *palos.*" Pally departed as strangely and quickly as he came.

The starch mango tree was decorated with jewels. The tall healthy mango tree held dozens of large juicy red and yellow mouthwatering fruits.

Lal continued to sit under the shade of the starch mango tree long after Pally left. However, he was visibly disturbed as if he was contemplating Pally's suggestion. Man, I have nothing to lose, Lal convinced himself.

Early next morning, as the sun was starting to peep through the clear blue sky and the grass was still wet from the night's dew, Lal positioned himself in the open verandah outside Pundit Kumar's newly built flat-board house. He wanted to get there before anyone because he had important business to straighten out. It was traditional for people to pay a visit to Pundit Kumar before they made any major decisions for a small fee or a gift of a *dhoti* or two white vests or a *lota* and *taria* set. A short while later, Lal came out from Pundit Kumar's prayer room smiling. He quickly stuck his two index fingers in his fobs, chuckled a merry tune, and walked down the newly paved road feeling confident and happy with himself that he took his friend's advice. After all, Pally was the most respected and learned man in the village.

The sound of drumming and chanting could be heard emanating from the usually quiet village from early that Saturday. The villagers could hardly wait for the final stick fighting match. People started to gather from hours before the match to socialize with others from the surrounding villages and place their bets. Suddenly the drumming stopped and a deafening silence pierced the atmosphere as Lal threw his stick in the middle of the *gayelle*. Everyone patiently looked on to see who would challenge Lal even though in their hearts everyone knew it would be Johnny. A few minutes later Johnny jumped into the *gayelle* and started waving his stick high into the air. Uproar then silence. The two competitors shook hands and the *carray* began. *Plax, twax, plax, twax* could be heard amid the chant. This parrying continued with blows flying and men bobbing and weaving. The chantwells were singing the praises of their stick fighters, hoping to bring out the warrior spirit in their champion. Things were looking good. People were admiring the great skills of both competitors as they were lashing with style and blocking with equal amount of style as the *gatka* continued. This display of technique and physical prowess continued for a while. Signs of boredom started to show on the faces of the crowd and the chant began to die down.

"Blood, blood," someone shouted out. "Blood, blood. Oh gosh, Johnny on the ground." The drumming and chanting died down completely. Johnny slowly got up, wiped his forehead with his rough hand, and looked at the brick-red liquid. As if the sight of blood brought the realization of the moment to life, with eyes open wide he threw a heavy blow. The crowd went wild, some cheering and some opposing. The parrying, drumming, and chanting continued with skills and technique on display. Satisfaction seemed to light up the faces of the excited crowd as some blood splattered on the ground

In the end, Lal was on the ground out cold. Women started to gather and fan him in an attempt to resuscitate him. Blood kept pouring from the large gash on his forehead. The elders pressed in to try to stop the bleeding. Someone shouted from the crowd, "Get Nurse Beulah." Suddenly the crowd started to make a small clearing for old man Parson. He was holding Nurse Beulah's hand, dragging her through the curious crowd to the *gayelle*. She looked confused as to her role. All eyes looked on to see what Nurse Beulah would do, how she would handle this. This was her first time dealing with anything outside of the local health center. She stooped down, bent over Lal, and called out his name a few times. Then she placed her mouth on his and started to blow into his mouth and press on his chest. After a moment she shouted, "Get me a clean rag and some water." Polly instinctively pulled out her old cream rag from her bosom and handed it to her. Beulah was a shiny fair-skinned woman in her late thirties. Beulah was well respected in the village, all the young girls looked up to her. She was good-looking, educated, and came from a well-to-do family. She dipped the rag into the enamel bowl of water, gently squeezed some of the water out, and pressed it to the wound. This was repeated a few times, then she started to clean out the dried blood from the other parts of his body.

When he finally became conscious be was helped to his feet and given a cup of cold rainwater. He looked confused and disoriented. He was taken home by a few of the men and instructed to get some rest by Nurse Beulah. Many were surprised; many lost their hard-earned cash. That was it. Lal was defeated, and Johnny was declared the champion by the elders.

Lal did not come out until a few days later, but when he did he had one thing on his mind. He decided to pay his good friend Pally a visit. He could hardly wait to face Pally and deal with him. How he could do something like this, Lal thought to himself. It looked as if Pally was waiting for him. As Lal rode up the gravel path he found Pally smoothing out a *dabla*. Their eyes met and silence followed. Lal found that he could not say a word even though he had rehearsed many times in his troubled mind what he was going to say to Pally, how he was going cuss up his tail and let him have it. It was Pally who broke the silence, "So yuh let meh down, man. What really happen to yuh Saturday?"

Lal could not believe his ears. He was shocked out of his mind. "Wait, you have de belly to ask me that, but what hell I does see is you who tell me to go and get meh stick mounted. Yuh know I don't take no part in them thing, and stupid me listen to yuh and go by Pundit Kumar," Lal angrily countered when he was finally able to catch himself.

"Wait, wait, wait. When I tell yuh to go and get yuh *poui* mounted I mean by Papa Luscifus not Pundit Kumar. Everybody in the village know that when it comes to serious business Papa Luscifus is the man. Wait, that is why yuh lose the match? Oh lawd, ah now understand. You is something else. When you have a li'l house blessing oh a li'l *graha pooja* you could go by Kumar. But when the stakes high and yuh have serious business to take care of, yuh doh leave that to chance. Yuh go by Papa Luscifus de obeah, man."

INSANE FIRE

It could not have been later than nine o'clock as Drupatiee had just dropped Armit off to school and was slowly making her way back home thinking about washing all that dirty clothes. The loose pebbles of the unpaved road massaged her broad feet as she thought about Ravi's greasy coverall and Jai's concrete-covered clothes that she had to wash on the juking board. She had to fill water from the standpipe in front of Mr. Leon's house before she started the back-breaking task of washing. The sun was up and about doing her thing of illuminating the sleepy forgotten village of Kangawood. The perfume of the wild marigold and the colorful periwinkle fought hard against the horrid stench emanating from Mr. Pope's hog pen. This blasted man, cyar, clean he dam place, she thought to herself. She continued to talk to herself as she hastened her pace. I wonder what to cook for lunch today, *stuepes*. She was jolted from her self-musing by smoke in the distance. It smelled like cane burning, nothing unusual about that. Burning cane was a smell she'd grown up with. As a matter of fact, she looked forward to that scent. She and her siblings were responsible for a few cane fires themselves.

What was confusing was that the odor reeked of burning cane but the smoke told another story. They did not match Drupatiee's sensory images. When one grew in the heartland of the sugar industry one knows like the burnt *tawa* mark on the wrist if it was a cane fire or not. The smoke was thick, black, and heavy. It looked serious. Cane fires were fun. Children could not wait for the fire to go out—and they did naturally, most of the time—to run through the burnt field and feast. There was an unusual sweetness to the juice of the burnt cane. They had the opportunity to break any blackened yellow or red cane stalk without the hassle of the sharp prickles from the cane leaves scratching and cutting into their tender hands and feet. The children were not the only ones who looked forward to the dying embers of the field. The men could be seen with their dogs running through the fields looking for manicou or iguana. The next step was a spicy curry. The housewives would always take front before front take them. They would pick fresh seasoning from the yard and grind it using their *sil* and *lorha* in preparation for when their husbands return to season up the loot. Every good *dulahin* knows that the secret to a finger-licking curry was a good fresh grind season. Every household always had fresh *bandhania*, chive, celery, *pudina*, fine-leaf and broad-leaf thyme, bird pepper, and hot pepper growing within arm's reach of the kitchen.

The smoke was thicker now and rising fast in the west. Little did Drupatiee know that her house was on fire and her life would forever be changed. Her tiny wooden cottage was totally engulfed in flames by the time she reached home. Her heart sank. She saw the neighbors scurrying about with buckets and pans trying to put the fire out while her husband and son stood like statues mounted on its hinge. After a long while, the only words that escaped Ravi's lips were, "I don't know what happen, I just don't know what happen." What was interesting was that the fire started in Ravi's garage and quickly spread to the old wooden house. The house was so old that the wood only served to feed the hungry monster so that it belched out red fury and coughed out blackened smoke. What started out as a routine Wednesday turned out to be an unforgettable Wednesday.

Drupatiee's days were all the same. Wake up at 4:00 a.m. to cook for the entire household. This meal would usually involve *sada roti*, steamed fluffy white rice, and some sort of curry or stew that could be eaten with both the rice and the roti. Next was waking up her husband and the children. Rosie had to wake up at five as she had to catch the six-o'clock bus. She was a form six student of the St. Joseph convent, so Drupatiee had to pack her lunch and get her organized in order to catch the bus. She would stand with Rosie by road until the old green Mazda van came. Only when Rosie was safe inside and the van was completely out of sight would Drupatiee return inside to continue the morning routine.

The next item on Drupatiee's agenda was waking up the boys and getting them organized for school. This was no easy task as you could hear Drupatiee's dragging voice echoing loudly over the other mothers to get the boys up and dressed on time. But they were Drupatiee's pride and joy. Amrit and Jai were twins and two years Rosie's junior. Unlike Rosie, they hated school and always looked for an excuse not to go. After organizing Rosie and the boys came the hardest task of all: organizing Ravi's breakfast. Cooking breakfast was not good enough for Ravi. She had to take out his breakfast and take it to him in the hammock in the back shed, wait until he'd tasted it to see if he wanted extra salt or some lime pepper sauce, *anchar*, or *kutchela*. Only when Ravi was satisfied could she go on to do her chores. If not, chores had to be halted. When the king was okay then she would sweep the never-ending dirt yard using a long yellowish-brown coconut broom. Next, it was off to clean the kitchen and wash the dishes and sweep the house. Only when these chores were completed would Drupatiee settle down to eat her breakfast. When she finished her breakfast—or most of the time, while she was still chewing her food—she would start the task of preparing the next meal. Her husband, Ravi, ran a small mechanic garage in a shed adjoining the old wooden house. It was known on the outside as a mechanic garage but everyone knew that he did the little odd electrical on vehicles every now and again.

Something went wrong, so wrong that morning, and what started as a small controllable electrical fire turned into a house fire and then the once lush, verdant cane stalks went up in flames. That was just what a decent hardworking family needed to create a fissure that would only widen with time and more tragedy. They had no choice but to move in for a few days with Drupatiee's younger sister, Lah, and her children. Lah and Drupatiee were very close as they were a year apart. As soon as the news reached Lah she arrived on the smoky scene trying to comfort her visibly distraught sister. "You, Ravi, and the children must come and stay with me and the children for a few days until you get back on your feet," Lah insisted.

"Well, just for a few days until we could build back something to live in," the slow heavy words managed to escape Drupatiee's chapped lips.

Lah was a smooth, dark, beautiful woman with thick long jet-black hair to complement her petite but shapely physique. She was the feistiest woman in the village, hence the reason she got the prime bachelor from the village. All the young ladies from her village as well as the surrounding villages had their eyes on Hanif. He was as rich as he was handsome. His muscular build complemented his ruddy complexion and rugged appearance. However, Lah had worked her saucy charm and brought the giant of a man to his knees. He was in front of Rokmin and Roshan's newly painted wooden house late one August night on both knees, begging them to marry Lah. Mind you, she had many suitors as well. The men say she

12

was as sweet as she was black. A wedding beyond the villagers' minds was held to celebrate the union of this couple. *Lavish* and *full of flair* were the only descriptors of these nuptials. Their spicy romance produced two children, Renata and Chandy. It was rumored that they both had secret acts of indiscretion. The one thing that was a fact was their undying love for each other. They never walked the village without holding on to each other. Hanif never came home without bringing a treat for his lover. They children were well cared for both physically and psychologically as they were both loving and nurturing parents and Hanif had the resources to meet their material needs. This was admired by almost all in the village as most people could barely afford to feed their children, far less to spoil them.

Hanif had recently passed away from a freak accident. He was a fisherman and the owner of three boats named after his wife and two daughters. What was amazing was that he had just returned from being at sea for three days, endured a violent storm with high winds and choppy waters, and finally made it back to land safely when a coconut tree fell on him. He spent thirteen days unconscious at the San Fernando General Hospital before he finally lost the fight. Lah was understandably heartbroken and devastated even though his death was expected by all. She had lost her longtime lover, her children's father, a good friend, and the only breadwinner of the household.

What was supposed to be a few days with Lah and her kids turned out to be three years. Lah was happy for her sister's company and her kids were excited to spend time with their cousins. Lah was also happy to have Ravi's help and advice in managing the business. This gave her the break she needed to relax and enjoy spending time with her new extended family. Both sisters would stay up late reminiscing about their childhood experiences. They also spent lots of time cooking and baking their favorite childhood foods and snacks.

Ravi immensely enjoyed working with Lah, helping her with the management and payment of the employees as well as the purchasing of equipment and supplies, and Lah ensured that he was handsomely remunerated. He enjoyed this new field of work. It took him out of exerting manual labor to the autonomy of managing big, strong men. He felt important and asserted his authority every chance he got even when it was not necessary. They had plenty of late-night discussions about the business. Most of the time Drupatiee would stay up with them and put in her two cents; however, when it got to the stage where technical jargon was necessary, she would excuse herself to get the coffee and any light snacks she and Lah had prepared earlier in the day. "I think this is where I get something to eat and something to drink," she would calmly say and exit to the kitchen. She would return with treats and shortly thereafter would call it a night. It was during one of these late-night discussions about the restructuring of the business that something went wrong. Something inside Ravi was awakened and could not be tamed. He was seeing his faithful aging wife juxtaposed against her beautiful younger sister. An affection was building in Ravi's heart for his forbidden sister-in-law. He now noticed how extremely attractive Lah was and how simple and plain Drupatiee was, and how she had aged in these few years. It was like he was seeing Lah for the first time. He could hardly believe how this beautiful specimen was still unmarried. "You look stressed. I think you need a neck rub," Ravi whispered during one discussion.

"Nah, I good, just a little tired from seeing all these figures," was her abrupt response. She felt something too, something wonderful but scary, so she was afraid to give it any life. Night after night, Ravi lay next to his wife but yearned for her sister. He would make love to his wife but imagine it was her sister. He thought about making passionate love to Lah. He thought about gently caressing her dark, smooth skin, licking the nape of her neck, and nibbling her tiny ears. These thoughts flooded his mind nightly that he became sick with obsession. Ravi fought hard to hold back his emotions. He thought about his faithful wife, his wonderful children, especially his gem of a daughter, his in-laws, his parents, and most of all, what the villagers would say. Many nights he spent turning and tossing, haunted by his love or lust for Lah. Drupatiee thought it was just the stress of the business as well as trying to rebuild and start again that plagued his sleep. "Ah tell yuh don't worry about anything, we will get through this," Drupatiee whispered in Ravi's ear as he tried to get comfortable.

"I can't help it. I have too much on my mind, fixing back the house, Rosie's exam coming up soon, and she needs to get textbooks, and the boys not going to school," Ravi softly and slowly uttered as if he was trying to convince himself more than Drupatiee that he was bothered about his family.

No matter how hard both Ravi and Lah tried to fight their unorthodox passion, their lives were connected by geography and occupation. Since both Ravi and Lah seemed starved for affection, it was only a matter of time before a volcanic eruption of romance exploded. Everyone in the village seemed to recognize the sparks between them, even the children, except Drupatiee.

The sparks fired between Lah and Ravi evolved into a huge inferno. Again, it seemed that everybody in the village knew about this hot affair except Drupatiee. It appeared that she refused to acknowledge it as the signs were so flagrant. Life went on as usual with this happy extended family. Business prospered, the children excelled, and all seemed well. It was almost a year later that Drupatiee finally acknowledged her husband's affair with her sister. Her reaction was the strangest thing. She sat in silence for a few minutes with a blank, stoic expression on her face and a cold, calculating look in her eyes. The few people around her thought that she had gone mad. After a few moments, she got up and left the house, walked into the yard through the huge arch gates, and headed down the road. She was last seen by villagers walking toward the pond. It could not have been later than 9:00 p.m.

THE FRIENDSHIP

Joe looked at Ben and he knew what the plan was. Ben's eyes lit up and a broad smile came over his round face. The unspoken message between them was normal; it was how they communicated. It had taken years of beautiful friendship to develop. They both waited until no one was around and then veered off the main road into the dirt track that led to Mr. Johnson's garden. The journey to the garden was therapeutic. The lush, verdant bushes seemed so friendly and waved to them as they passed by. Joe and his best friend, Ben, walk through the bushes in silence, enjoying the liberation until they reached Ben's grandfather's garden shed. The birds, butterflies, and bees seemed to be frolicking as their sound and sight punctuated the landscape. Both teenagers spent a lot of time in the garden. They enjoyed each other company and spending time in the garden was their personal space to do so. It was peaceful and serene. There was always plenty to see and do. The outer perimeter of the garden was enclosed by fruit trees, so there was always something to make chow with.

Ben and Joe lived in the same rural village. As a matter of fact, they were neighbors. They were about the same age, attended the same school, and had the same friends. However, Ben appeared to be the more courageous and daring one. He was the instigator of all their rendezvous. Strangely Joe seemed never to need any convincing, he was always on board. Joe trusted Ben's judgment. One day Ben suggested to his best friend that life must be more than just going to school and doing chores. "What you think about a break from school today?" Ben said.

"What you had in mind?" Joe quickly responded.

"I have a plan that is foolproof, no one will ever find out," Ben continued

"Okay, well, let me hear yuh," was Joe's counter. And that was the start of many days of absence from school and visits to Mr. Johnson's garden. They both hated school, so they passed most of their school days at the old garden shed in tranquility. Fun was a big part of their day. There were the trees to climb, the river to explore, open fields to run through, the fruits to pick, meals to prepare, chow to make, and games to play. What more could any teenager want than to be left alone to roam and discover the world through his own eyes at his own pace?

Mr. Johnson was always happy to have them; he immensely enjoyed their company. As a matter of fact, when he had an inkling that they were coming he would prepare extra for lunch. Mr. Johnson lived alone in the village as his ailing wife had passed two years earlier. His three children were grown and had families of their own. His youngest son, Benjamin, Ben's father, lived at the other end of the village. So Mr. Johnson found himself spending more time than usual in his garden. His garden was not only his main source of income but a way of escape from the ominous depression. As soon as Mr. Johnson saw the boys coming he would blurt out, "What chow we making today, fellars?" They would both smile, knowing they were welcomed. Mr. Johnson would ask in a halfhearted manner, "So no school today, boy?" He took what they said and never bothered to investigate, even though from his years of experience he could tell that they were less than truthful. It was always one of the same three old excuses they would give him: no water, toilets not working, and teachers having a meeting. Mr. Johnson never bothered to even bring up the subject in a conversation with the boys' parents when he met them at the usual Sunday mass. As a matter of fact, he kept their visits to his garden as a secret.

Rarely would he ask them for help. He just enjoyed watching them climb, fish, bathe in the cool, refreshing muddy water, and reminisce about his own childhood. Both boys had clothes hidden in the garden shed and they always made sure that after their long hours in the river they left them hanging on the rusty galvanized fence to dry. It was as if their presence brought a new joy into Mr. Johnson's heart. Even though one of the boys was is grandson, he never treated them differently. He expressed the same affection for both Ben and Joe. Today now no different. When they had their fill and hunger was starting to grip them, Ben inquired of Papa, "So what we cooking today?"

"Fish and rice," was Papa's gleeful response. The boys quickly went to the manmade pond at the back of the garden shed and fished out some *cascadura*, cleaned and seasoned them. Papa instructed them step-by-step on how to prepare the curry, and soon the pot was bubbling. The spicy smell of curry floated through the garden. The meals were always delicious. It was prepared on an open fire made by placing three rough river stones in a triangular formation and placing dried sticks and twigs at the open end of the base of the triangle. They laughed heartily as they gobbled up the smoky feast of curried *cascadura* with coconut milk and sappy white rice.

"Who could imagine that it was more than fifty years ago that we used to spend most of our time in this same garden shed?" Ben slowly said as he lifted the *cascadura* to his mouth and took a small bite of the white meat. His brown eyes brightened and a wicked smile came over his wrinkled face. The curry sauce dripped down Joe's shaking wrist and a beautiful smile flashed across his face only for a moment.

"I know, who could ever imagine," was Joe's response as he slowly ate his curried *cascadura* with coconut milk and sappy white rice.

THE SCARLET IBIS

I rushed outside the vehicle to view this specular sight. Looking at the sunset always made me feel relaxed and calm. I watched as the orange ball of fire slowly disappeared behind the horizon and the scarlet ibis hurried to their home in the Caroni Swamp. There were birds of every kind and color chirping harmoniously in perfect synchronization, but I paid them no attention. I only had eyes for the bright red. I was in love with their color, their flight, their habitat, everything about them. The way they flew in such synchronization, and the few cattle egret between just lent contrast to create the most amazing and breathtaking sight. Clouds of red just bursting and spilling in one direction, leaving nothing but peace in their path. The savage chilly winds nipped at my ears and nose. I was not clothed for the weather. Why was it so cold and chilly at this time of the year? I reasoned. The muddy waters were teaming with life and energy

The swamp always captivated and held me in rapt attention. The brown stagnant water held so much mystery, and every now and again the head of a caiman would pop up, breaking the enigma. Now tiny lights began to flicker as the crab catchers walked to the edge of the river hoping to fill their bags. The flambeaux started emerging and so too the noise. The tranquility was broken by children screaming, men laughing and knocking glasses, and women knocking spoons against pots. However, this was not unusual. The bird sanctuary was always buzzing with activities on a Friday and Saturday afternoon. Families came to relax, bathe, catch crab, and have a good time. For me, it was always about the experience. The sight blew me away. My mother was always upset with me when I refused to spend time with my family and catch crab or fish. I preferred to gaze into the sunset or admire one of the ten wonders of my world, the scarlet ibis in flight.

My family had been visiting this same spot for as long as I could remember. Sometimes to fish, sometimes to catch crabs, and sometimes just to relax. So I grew up absorbing the amazing sunset and the stunning scarlet ibis flying home. I felt rejuvenated, reborn whenever I saw the huge flaming, gigantic ball of liquid gold making its way below the ocean to rest for the night. Beautiful thoughts and fresh new ideas rushed into my mind as if they were all trying to get my undivided attention at the same time. The neat formation of the scarlet ibis fluttering their graceful wings over my head always brought just deep peace to my soul and amazement to my heart. I could stand for hours after the sun had set and the birds had flown away just contemplating the serenity and replaying the sight.

The sandflies and mosquitoes were now cutting into skin, feasting on fresh blood. The smell of curry, barbeque, and fish broth confused the senses as it permeated the atmosphere. The fireflies flicked their on-and-off switch a thousand times a minute. The activity of fishing and crab-catching held no intrigue for me. I went back into the vehicle and continued to read my book, *To Kill a Mockingbird*. I was known as the bookworm in the family as I would get lost in my books. I loved to read and would spend all my free time reading. I was introduced to reading by my next-door neighbor Perl. She would lend me different books she was reading. Perl was a form-five secondary-school student and was a bookworm herself. One day I saw her reading a book under the laden rose mango tree. "What is that you reading? You seemed lost in it," I called out.

"A juicy story," Perl said, smiling, without lifting her head from the book. "I would lend it to you when I am finished," she said, still smiling. Perl really kept true to her word, and so began my journey of no return into the land of books. I was curious to know what had Perl so engrossed. It was *Wuthering Heights.* I developed an insatiable thirst for something different from my own way of life. It was my way to travel to different worlds and share in different peoples' experiences. I incalculably enjoyed this experience. It brought me enormous bliss amid my perplexing life.

When the fish broth was ready, my mother called me to come and get my food. She took out my food, handed me the steaming bowl of broth, and motioned to me to sit on the brick next to my younger brother. The green okra floating on top of the whitish sauce slid from side to side as I tried to balance the enamel bowl and my book and drink. I headed back to the car to continue my journey into the world of Atticus Finch. As I started to explore the racism faced by Tom Robinson, my blood boiled at unknown temperatures. My anger was broken by screams coming from the river's edge. My father and brothers had gone out a little way into the fiver to fish, so my mind immediately went in that direction. I could not understand what all the commotion was about. I jumped out of the car and raced toward my family. I saw everyone looking into the darkness and speaking frantically. As I looked into the river trying to figure out what was wrong, I could see nothing but thick darkness.

My mother retold how my father and two older brothers had gone grouper fishing in an inflatable dinghy a little distance into the swamp. She continued to say how she kept looking at the light in the boat and suddenly the tiny vessel overturned and the flambeaux went out. On hearing this I clutched my book tightly to my chest and closed my eyes and repeated Psalms 23. My father was a very good swimmer and so too were my brothers, so I was not too, too worried. I knew that soon I would see them swimming ashore or paddling back on their dinghy. More people started to gather and offer comfort and advice. An old fat man ran to his truck and returned with a large flashlight. "This would do the trick," he said as he flashed this bright light into the water and combed the river from right to left repeatedly. Everyone looked anxiously but nothing was in sight.

By this time everyone had halted their activities and joined in. Soon another little wooden boat went out into the darkness with my uncle and two men we did not know. Hours had passed and still no sight of my father, brothers, or the orange dinghy. Other relatives soon arrived at the swamp. Somehow, somebody was able to convince my mother to take the kids and return home. I was mad as a bull. I wanted to stay and see my father and brothers swimming ashore and tell everyone, "You see, I knew that they would be okay"—and besides, my vision was better than anyone's. After all, I could read in the dark for long periods of time. I knew I would be able to see something somebody had missed. I fell off to sleep for a bit with my book still in my hands. When I opened my eyes after what felt like an eternity I noticed that no one was around but the place was noisy. I ran outside to see my father and brothers having something to eat. This sight warmed my heart. But I'd known that nothing was going to happen and that they would return to us safely. My father and brothers managed to swim until they were rescued by a fishing vessel. Their dinghy strangely capsized, and because there was no light, it made it difficult for them to navigate, having no sense of geography. So they swam to the mangrove and were rescued by the first light of the new day.

It was almost two years before we visited the Caroni Swamp again. It held no painful memories for me. I was excited to go as I wanted to become one with the sunset and the scarlet ibis. My mother never allowed any adventure into the murky waters no matter how appealing the request was or who it came from. "Fishing from the bank is allowed, crab catching in the mangrove is allowed, end of story," she would roughly say. I was exultant to be at the swamp and soak in the wonders of my world. I looked on with incredulity as the sweltering globe vanished, leaving smudges of gold in its path. The breathtaking sight of the scarlet ibis captured me and pulled me in. The majestic creatures gracefully made their way home, flying in sync with each other and my heart. I stood in awe.

THE CHINESE MANGO

"Better hurry up, closing five minutes," Chin said in fast but broken syllables. My mother, along with the few other customers, scrambled to get her last few items. My mother loved shopping at Chin's grocery. "Yuh could get everything yuh want in one place: grocery, market, clothes, wares, and even hardware things," she would say. Chin was one of two supermarkets in Longdenville. As the sun slowly began to dip behind the horizon to hide for the night, Mr. Chin started to clean and pack up the supermarket. Mr. Chin came from a long line of immigrants who controlled the dry goods and laundry business. He never socialized much with the villagers except in the context of business, hence his English was poor, making it difficult to understand him. Most people spoke to him in a combination of sign language and two-word sentences. Sometimes his pronunciation was so off base that only gesticulation could solve the shoppers' mystery. Mr. Chin was in his mid-eighties. He always wore rumpled ill-fitting clothes and a pair of dirty clogs. His nails were overgrown and dirty, and his straight jet-black hair fell untidily to the side of his wrinkled round face.

I loved going on errands at Chin's for my mother. I always came back with the wrong items and had to make several trips. Each trip meant a piece of dried salty mango. Above where Chin sat collecting payments were two shelves with huge glass jars containing preserved fruits of every color, size, and shape. There were the black pepper prunes, the black sweet prunes, the white prunes, the red pepper plums and mango, the red sweet mango, but the best was the dried, orange salty mango. Just looking at it made my mouth water. Whenever my mother bought that particular preserved fruit, we would only get one piece each as it had to be shared among six children. The first item we would run to the shop to purchase

23

was this mouthwatering dried preserved mango. Whenever we received money from visiting relatives on special occasions or earned it from doing chores around the neighborhood, straight to Chin we went. My sister and I would repeatedly rub the orange mango on our lips to give the illusion of lipstick. We savored every bit of it. The anticipation of Chin slowly opening the lid of the jar, removing one piece of mango at a time with partially rusty tongs, and placing them on squares of brown paper made us dizzy.

The taste of the dried salty mango was pure happiness. We had to get more of this happiness. "Want to find out how you could get as much mango as you want?" Garvin whispered in my ear."

"Of course," I excitedly answered back. So we hatched a plan to get Chin out of the shop. Chin never left the shop even though he lived upstairs with his wife, daughter, and two grandsons. His meals were always brought down to him by his wife or his grandsons, Luke and Chen. His daughter worked all the way in Port of Spain in some government office. Well, as for her husband, nothing is known about him. Some say he went back to China. His family was rarely seen in the shop but he never left the shop. We knew the boys as they went to school with us. Luke was in my class and Chen was in my brother's class. They never had any dealings with us. As a matter of fact, they had no dealings with anyone. They just went to school and back home. However, every day they would go home for lunch. They were by far the brightest kids in school.

My brother, Garvin, was a master at planning and executing heists flawlessly. He was four years my senior, tall with bright black eyes, curly hair, and a friendly personality. We were best friends. The thought of getting my hands on this happiness haunted me night and day. I always wondered if Luke and his brother ate any of the preserved fruits from their grandfather's shop. I imagined that they could just take anything they wanted, as much as they wanted. I would always look at Luke's fingers and lips to see if there were any residual orange stains, but there were none. I could not take it any longer, so on our way from school one day I walked up to Luke. "Do you ever eat any of that dried salty preserved mango from your grandfather's shop?" I inquired.

"What? No. Why?" was his response with a confused look on his yellow face. He appeared upset and his eyes seemed to get smaller.

"I just wanted to know. If that was my shop, I would eat it every day," was my friendly response.

"Well, it is not your shop," he rudely blurted out. Luke is such a backside, I grumbled to myself. I waited until he was a good way off and shouted out, "Chinese, Chinese, never die. Flat nose and chinky eyes." I knew if my mother found out she would kill me, but I did not care. How could he be so rude when I was just making friendly conversation with him? I reasoned.

The plan was to set the old abandoned wooden house next door to Chin's grocery on fire. When Chin notices the fire, he would run outside to try to put the fire out. Then we would run in, grab a handful of the orange delight, and put it in our pockets. We would obliviously be dressed to facilitate this, and then calmly walk outside and join the gathering crowd. Since everyone would be caught up trying to put the fire out, no one would suspect us. This was a master plan. Garvin had to be a genius. And since no one was living in the house, our deeds would not be considered bad. As a matter of fact, we would be helping out the community by removing that unsightly building.

Everything was set and we put our master plan into motion. What we did not estimate was the strength and direction of the wind. The old house soon went up in flames as expected but no one seemed to notice. The small fire continued until it caught on to Chin's small storeroom adjoining his house, and still no one noticed. I was getting scared now. Garvin's bright black eyes widened in shock. The fire began to blaze and crackle, and soon Chin's house caught on fire. The house was old and the weather was hot and the wind was strong. The sight was devastating. It all happened so fast. The crackling sound of fire could be heard from afar and huge columns of smoke started to rise quickly into the even sky. The house was engulfed in flames, with burning debris falling all around.

A crowd started to gather. People were busy running back and forth, pouring buckets of water on the fire. But the more water they poured, the worst the fire grew. The two old rusty barrels of kerosene and the many kegs of cooking oil fed the hungry fire. The villagers were running, trying to get Chin's wife and grandsons out of the inferno. Some were also trying to salvage what they could. My heart was now beating at an unreasonable pace. Hot tears began rolling down my lean cheeks. My brother tried to comfort me but he looked like he needed to be comforted as well. We cried softly as the fires roared loudly. We were a wreck. Hundreds of what-ifs punctuated my troubled mind. "My mother would kill us" was the dominating one.

When the dust settled, Chin's grocery that my mother loved to shop at was no more. And my brother, Gavin, and I never placed salty mango anywhere close to our mouths again. What happened over the next two years was difficult for me to witness. I daily had to look at Chin and his family rebuild their home and business. They constructed a two-room makeshift house and a little shed that now served as the grocery. From this, they operated their lives and business. Gavin and I never spoke of what we did, not even when we were alone. I was afraid to even think of our irresponsible behavior fueled by our juvenile voracity. I always made an effort to be nice to Luke and his brother. I carried the hefty weight of guilt with me daily. Within that time, Luke and I became friends as he had no other friends. We would walk home together and he would sometimes offer to help me with my algebra homework. One day I offered to help him with his *Divial* project as he was having trouble sourcing the information. The next morning he stopped by my house on his way to school. He waited until I was done, then we walked up the peaceful, overgrown road together. The early morning sun filtered through the trees and shimmered on the rough asphalt, creating a beautiful feeling. The air seemed fresher than usual and the birds sang sweeter. Things were definitely getting better. The guilt was becoming less and less. I had less and less trouble sleeping or running errands for my mother at Chin's.

Luke slipped his hands into his right pocket and pulled out a brown package and handed it to me. I was excited. It was not my birthday or Christmas, and absolutely no one had ever given me a present besides on those two occasions. A shy "thank you" rolled off my lips and a broad smile came over my face as I ripped the package open. A partial smile was also beginning to appear on Luke's shiny round face. I was dumbfounded. I could not believe it. My eyes rolled back in their sockets and my smiled quickly turned to anguish. It was my once-favorite dried, orange, salty preserved mango.

CORN SOUP QUEEN

"Corn soup, *geera* gizzard, and souse, only ten dollars a cup, the best in town," the sign said in badly formed letters. "The usual," Melda said, smiling as she chirped to the tune of Georgy Isaac's "Night Nurse." Melda was the corn soup queen. She loved corn soup, and so every Saturday night she would make her way to the junction to enjoy Ms. Jean and son's corn soup with shadow *beni* sauce. The smell was inviting, the look appealing, and the taste was worth the wait in line. The yellow pieces of corn amid the orange carrot, green okra, white dumpling, and pink pigtail summoned even the passersby. Melda could not resist a Friday nightline, a hot spicy cup of corn soup, and two cold beers. She had become good friends with Ms. Jean by being a regular customer. As soon as Ms. Jean saw Melda, she would start preparing her order, because Melda's order was the same from the time Ms. Jean started selling at the junction. Ms. Jean started off about seventeen years ago selling boiled corn on a Saturday night to earn some extra cash to feed seven hungry mouths. Business was slow, but Ms. Jean kept coming back week after week. Not in an effort to influence the villagers' lifestyle but to feed hungry mouths. However, she accomplished both. A few years later her son, Gilbert, joined her with an addition to the menu with his famous souse. The souse was an instant hit with the men, so they kept asking for other things to eat, especially when they were intoxicated. Things evolved and the next thing, there was geera gizzard, souse, and corn soup every month end on Friday and Saturday nights. If there was a holiday on Monday, they would be there on Sunday night as well.

The community enjoyed this addition. It encouraged others to become more enterprising. Bagoo moved his doubles stall from behind the market to next to Ms. Jean. Jeff started up a small oyster thing, and Vida started frying *pholourie* hot on the spot. These delicacies encouraged villagers to socialize, and this start of commerce brought a new way of life to this rural farming community—a way of life that they all embraced wholeheartedly. Young and old looked forward to every month end. Lining out of their homes late at night and buying food was new to them but they loved it, especially the young adults and housewives. Tired housewives did not have to hustle after a hard day of taking care of children to prepare dinner, and young adults got the chance to socialize with friends and members of the opposite sex. This was a win-win for everybody, thanks to Ms. Jean, Bagoo, Vida, and Jeff.

Meld and Boyboy were almost to the front of the line when a fight erupted. No one knew exactly how the fight started, but people started to gather and noise erupted into chaos. A huge circle formed without any instructions. There was a clearing in the circle and several persons were on the ground, each of them trying to injure the other. The pot of corn soup and souse went flying into the air as somebody's hand hit the leg of Ms. Jean's unstable table. All Melda felt was a hot sprinkler being turned on. Pieces of corn and gizzard littered the pavement and road. When the dust cleared, Melda found herself at the San Fernando General Hospital with a broken leg and some surface bruises. The visits from the villagers cheered her up, especially a cup of Ms. Jean's corn soup. She spent four days there and was eventually sent home to recuperate. But this did not stop the lining on weekends. As a matter of fact, people from other nearby villages made their way every Friday and Saturday night to Caratal to share in the excitement.

As soon as Melda was able to walk freely on her own she was back at Lookman Junction. She did not need to join the line, which was always long. She was given celebrity status. As soon as someone noticed Melda coming down the road, a special stool was provided for her at the side of Ms. Jean's table. "One cup of corn soup with *shado beni* sauce and medium pepper for you," Gilbert would tease, handing her the steaming cup. Gilbert loved to see Melda feast on the soup. She sipped the sauce and daintily nibbled the kernels off the ear, and slowly chewed the dumplings and vegetables. Melda ate her corn soup and asked for another. She was happy to be out and among her villagers. She enjoyed the ambience, the people, the music, the noise, the smell, the madness. She could not imagine life without this avenue for relaxation. She began to question herself how did she manage for those eight weeks.

The villagers were happy to see Melda out and enjoying the evening. She glowed in her white pants and fiery red top. Everyone came to say hello to her. The line to greet her was just as long as the corn soup line. Vida sent over a bag of hot *pholourie* and a cold Solo soft drink. She giggled as she bit into the fluffy ball. She swayed from side to side, enjoying the music, the food, and the company. She reflected on how happy she was and how lucky she was to have good friends and neighbors. As the evening turned into night, the few people turned into a crowd. The music became louder and excitement was high in the air. It was a beautiful moonlit night with cool air, but no one noticed. The night creatures came out but no one noticed. The euphoria of this new culture entangled everyone.

The jubilation came to a halt as high screams covered the music and objects flew up in the air. Some of the people could be seen running in different directions, while others were running to Ms. Jean's stall. Noises and chaos were good indicators as to what was happening. As if on cue a large mass began forming. And guess who was in the middle of the ground covered in her favorite corn soup? When the dust cleared, Melda was left injured with a broken leg. Melda was truly the corn soup queen.

THE MYSTERY OF
THE MANGROVE

The thick black mud gave off a putrid odor but Bhalna plodded along, sticking his huge, black hand into the holes, trying to outwit the tiny creatures. The mosquitoes buzzed romantically in his ears, causing his thoughts to race over four decades. Sometimes he would laugh at this buzzing and other times he would become very annoyed. It was almost 4:00 a.m., and his bag was still empty. He remembered his mother's story about the mosquito being the greatest lover in the insect world. She said that only someone who was madly in love with another would so persistently whisper in the person's ears, "I love you, I love you." The atmosphere was still and the darkness was giving way to the dawning of a new day. The dew-laden branches brushed against his cheeks, causing him to constantly wipe his face on the collar of his old plaid shirt. How was he going to pay his bills? Six children to feed, a loving wife, and a sick mother. What was he going to do? He'd had many of these low days but it was never this bad. A feeling of depression filled his soul. The nagging kind that would creep up from time to time to steal whatever little joy life was kind enough to share with him.

The red, black, and white mangroves surrounded Bhalna and a clear sky covered him. Ordinarily, this should give one a sense of security and comfort, but the opposite was true for Bhalna. This setting made him a little afraid, and that was good because it caused him to recite the mantra his pundit had given him. It's been almost seven years now but he still could not get over the death of his eldest son right there in the mangrove. He wished he did not have to go to the mangroves but it was necessary to feed his family. The money from construction was little, not fixed, and seasonal. Only when people got paid did they pay him. He could not support a family of nine on promises, so crab catching was like his primary occupation except it was only done on evenings—laughable one would think.

A million burning balls of light hung overhead as one giant white rock floated over the abyss. It was peaceful except for the persistent whispering of "I love you, I love you" of the mosquitoes. The wild fireflies were definitely a help, not only with the lighting but they also enhanced the ambience. "Yuh know this could be a romantic play minus the smell and the mosquitoes," he jokingly said to himself.

Bhalna's life was complicated like the mangrove. Problems seemed to constantly prop up around him like the roots of the rare white mangrove that grew above the earth's surface, and his debts just increased like the red mangrove roots that extend from the leaves of the tree to the ground. For him, life was one colossal irony. The harder you worked, the poorer you got. And the least you worked, the richer you became.

Pooran had gone into the mangroves with three of his school friends to hunt iguanas but never returned. So many stories were told, but all had more holes than the very mangrove he was in—irony of ironies. The police must have gotten paid off, according to Diptee. "Money talks and bullshit walks," was her comment whenever anyone brought the subject up. All the evidence pointed to his friends' negligence, but the police still could not make an arrest. "*Chupidness*," she would say. "If ah had some money yuh would ah see how fast they would ah catch de murderers. Them dutiness and them god will deal with them," she would end with whenever anyone was brave enough to engage the topic.

As Bhalna put the nip of puncheon rum to his mouth and took a sip, he heard a familiar sound. "Pa, Pa," Pooran's high-pitched voice called out his name. The voice kept calling out to Bhalna, the sound coming from the opposite direction. Without thinking he followed the voice. It led him farther and farther into the dark, thorny mangrove as if he had lost all sense of wise judgment. While the night air was cold, he felt hot. While the mangrove was a scary place, he felt comforted for some unusual reason. He followed the voice for a few more minutes until he saw a huge bright light in the darkness. It was so bright that Bhalna had to cover his eyes. Something unusual happened in the middle of the mangrove that only he and Diptee know about up until this day. He could not describe what happened, but just then a stroke of good luck stuck him. As if the gods had been listening to his whining and complaining, within half an hour his two bags were filled with crabs and his heart was emptied of its pain. He had finally outwitted the crabs, the system, and most importantly his greatest enemy, his mind. He dragged the heavy bags out of the mangrove, enduring the poking and scraping from the protruding legs of the crabs because he now possessed new physical and psychological fortitude. Money was not the only benefit of the mangrove now. He could hardly wait to share the secret of what transpired in the mangrove with his high-school lover. He remembered a time twenty-seven years ago when he could hardly wait to share what he considered the best news with Diptee. His family had not only consented but also agreed on a date for the wedding, and a smirk came over his face and speed in his steps. A good curried crab and dumpling were definitely going to be dinner later. Cold *mauby* to wash it down and a good backrub. What more a man could want in this one day? Bhalna comforted himself with these thoughts. He loaded his two bags onto his bicycle and excitedly rode home before the sun decided to return vengeance on the inhabitants. Sharing his secret, a hot cup of coffee, a piece of *roti* with some *alloo choka*, and a good sleep were the only things on his mind now.

Diptee, like her husband and mother-in-law, still could not get over Pooran's death. It just did not make sense to her. It went against the natural order of things. How is a mother supposed to bury her child? Children are supposed to bury their parents. Pooran's death left her robotic. She did her chores as if she was on autopilot. The house and the yard were always well cleaned, fresh food was always prepared, the children well groomed, and everything was perfect. There was no point in which she could be found wanting. However, the spark in her brown eyes had gone out, the smile on her face disappeared, and the spice in her voice was absent. She even stopped humming her *bhajans*, for which the boys were happy. She just existed because death was not ready for her, even though she was ready for him and would embrace him wholeheartedly. Her mother-in-law, while still visibly disturbed by her eldest grandson's death, tried to comfort her several times, but as usual, it would end in heavy waterworks for both of them, she never pursued the matter further.

Diptee was still *sakaying* a *roti* on the *chulah* when Bhalna entered the outside kitchen. She could hear him whistling from a distance and knew something was strange. It was an unusual day for the Dasine family as today made seven years since Pooran passed away. Bhalna was usually loud and demanding of breakfast, but today he was calm and whistling an old Indian film song. They all knew what day it was, so no one had to get any instruction to function. The boys had already taken the cows and goats out to graze across the river. Sandra was getting ready for school and the two smaller children were still asleep. Ma was sitting in the shed in her worn hammock, sipping coffee in her favorite enamel cup. Bhalna quietly walked up to Diptee and placed his arms around her skinny waist, kissed the *sindoor* on her forehead, and whispered something in her ear that forced a beautiful smile across her pale face.

"A-a, how yuh come home so late? Ah was expecting yuh since forday morning," Diptee lovingly said as if to say something for the sake of just saying it. She knew in her heart that all was well and nothing needed to be said.

Just for the sake of responding he softly replied, "Ghul, ah know wah you mean. Ah just want to spend some time with meh family today."

Their souls seemed so intimately knitted with each other that words were not necessary to communicate. Words were only used for the others around them. Their eyes spoke the magic of the language. Bhalna was wet with dew and dirty water, and the smell of rotting mud emanated from his clothes. But today this did not offend Diptee. She would usually scold him for entering the house in this condition. He had firm instructions to take his mangrove clothes off, shower outside with rainwater by the old barrel before entering the house. The early morning sun partnered with the wind, the birds, and insects to create a heavenly harmony. The smell of the atmosphere was fragranced with orange and lemon blossoms. The feeling of peacefulness was evident, and the sight of the sun shining down jewels on the village was glorious. Just a perfect day for anything. How could this once dreaded day hold so much peace and promise? God must really exist, Diptee reasoned to herself.

The mystery of the mangrove changed everything for the Dasine family. The family was finally able to put Pooran to rest and live again. They now had many great things to look forward to. Sandra was getting married to Premchand, the son of a well-respected businessman from Valsayn. This was going to be a big wedding and Premchand's family was paying for everything, including Sandra's wedding dress. A wedding that the entire extended family and village was looking forward to. Sammy passed his common entrance exam and was getting ready to attend Queen's Royal College. The two older sons, Armit and Anil, were in Canada picking apples. The last two girls were in doing well in primary school. The long, bitter tropical winter was ended and the autumn of the tropics was commencing. A beautiful season was unfolding like the *mussaenda* for the Dasines. Ma continued to sit in the shed and reminisce about her young days when dementia allowed her to. The magic returned to Diptee's eyes, the spice to her voice, and the pep in her step. She started humming her *bhajans* again, this time more frequently and louder. However, Bhalna never gave up his crab catching. Now he did it just for the love of it and to be close to his son. He stretched out on his hammock, picked his few remaining teeth with a matchstick, rubbed the couple of gray hairs on his chest, and smiled at Diptee as if to say the gods really do smile. She smiled back from her crocus bag hammock as if to say, "All is well, Bhalna." The magic language of love was spoken only through their eyes, and only these two pairs of eyes securely held the secret of the mangrove.

CARNIVAL QUEEN

Her huge thighs and vulgar bottom swayed from side to side as she wined to the rhythm of Calypso Rose, "Ah going down San Fernando." Francine was hot, a great dresser, and an even hotter dancer. She loved the night disco and never missed a party. She was known at all the popular nightclubs as the life of the party. She lit up the place. The young women hated her, but the young men and the old men adored her. She came alive for the carnival. It was her season. She immensely enjoyed the months leading up to the greatest show on earth. Francine attended every fete but J'ouvert was her life. She never missed a J'ouvert celebration. Early morning she could be seen coming down the hill, skimpily dressed but well smeared with a mud rainbow. She was always selected to model costumes from leading bands for the king and queen competition. Francine was voluptuous, had a small waist and bulging hips and bottom. These body parts would wiggle as she walked up the hill. Men would come outside of their houses just to look at her walk up the hill in her high heels, to the annoyance of their wives.

A fair, chubby kid with rosy cheeks and short picky hair, Francine blossomed into a swan. She grew up in the heart of the city of Laventille, Port of Spain. Her poor and underprivileged upbringing taught her to fight to survive, and not only to survive but to stand out. She grew up as an only child in a single-parent household. Her mother had no fixed income. She did odd jobs in the neighborhood as well as in Port of Spain to take care of herself and her daughter. She had no skills, so her options were limited to domestic work or janitorial work. These tasks engaged her for long unreasonable hours, sometimes even nights. "Now come and close the door. Go back and sleep, but make sure and wake up on time to go to school," Jean would say before leaving to go to the Port of Spain market to sweep. Francine was left alone most of the time to fend for herself. So waking up early to go to school was not a huge deal for Francine. Her primary school attendance was good, but when she entered secondary school things changed. She started missing a day a week, then a few days a month. Soon entire months she would be absent.

By the age of ten, she was popular among the community members, especially the boys. She spent most of her afternoon into night walking the streets and lining at the corner. She would often traverse the pan yard and mass camps offering to do chores for a small fee as a means of earning money to purchase the nice things she had an eye for. Many of the men she interacted and worked with also visited her house on the hill. This led to her loose and promiscuous lifestyle. The women disliked her for the way she flirted with their husbands in their presence, almost like they were invisible. She was introduced to exotic dancing on one of these many encounters at a nightclub. She found that she had a natural liking and talent for this lifestyle. She soon became the most famous exotic dancer in Port of Spain. Francine's reputation was now gaining momentum. It became a thing in the community for people to refer to a visit to the house on the hill when trying to say that the person was paying for pleasure. Her mother was old now and did not offer any resistance or display any disgust at her daughter's lifestyle. This annoyed the neighbors and caused them to keep away from her.

She continued to live alone in that same small house on top of the hill after her mother passed away. From there the sight was not only breathtaking but also gave a perfect view of what was going on in town. Many men passed through the doors of her house but none ever stayed longer than a week. Carnival was only months away, so Francine was primed and ready to display the queen costume for the band Hype. Her longtime suitor Mathew was playing mass with that said band. Matthew was constantly trying to woo her amid the heavy competition. That was what she appreciated about him. For years he had been her loyal suitor. He was five years younger than her but did not look it one bit. He was always right there to pick her up when things did not work out with her people, which very often happened. His parents and friends discouraged and cautioned him about her reputation as if he did not already know, but he only smiled. He was the calmest and most loving person in all of Laventille. What shocked everyone was how this quiet gem of a man could ever be attracted to this flamboyant, feisty woman.

Matthew was tall and slim, with large brown eyes that smiled before his lips did. His pleasant personality only complemented his handsome looks and stately physique. Like Francine, he was a sharp dresser. He worked as an accountant for a manufacturing company in San Juan but in his spare time, he built cupboards. This is how he really came to know Francine. He knew her from the area, and her reputation preceded her. Matthew had repaired some of her kitchen cupboards at no labor cost. He was immediately attracted to her and a friendship blossomed. Matthew fell in love with her but she would not commit as her socialization led her to choose the fellas that were just passing through town. Francine outright refused his expensive ring when Matthew proposed, telling him that rolling stones gather no moss. He was devastated but he never gave up. Old man Randolph used to say to Francine every time he saw her passing, "Ghul, why yuh doh get married and settle down? That boy really love yuh bad. Yuh playing hard to get, one day, one day he go catch yuh and put yuh in a cage." Many times after that Matthew asked Francine to marry him but the answer was always the same.

She was now living alone and in her fifties. She looked great. As the saying went, she became more beautiful with time like a good bush rum. She had lost some of her spunk but still had enough to captivate many men. She had a steady job now as a cashier at a fabric store in Port of Spain. She seemed different. The visits by men to the house on the hill became less and less. Then one day somebody realized that there were no more visitors. She made a conscious effort to be nice to the women and stopped her flirting with the married men.

The wedding of Matthew and Francine became a community affair. The community came together to cook the food and decorate the house on the hill. The women put their past feelings behind and came together to celebrate. Young and old came out to lend their support for this unusual union. What changed her mind, no one will ever know. Only that carnival Monday and Tuesday they'd played mass together and next thing people started receiving wedding invitations. Early Ash Wednesday, while most of Port of Spain was still covered in mist and the trees still heavy with dew, Matthew could be seen walking down the hill, leaving Francine smiling and waving in the gallery. The sun had not come up as yet and the street sweepers were busy getting rid of the remnants of the carnival. The hill air was fresh and the day beckoned invitingly to all to enjoy its bliss. Maybe it was the power of the carnival, as the old people used to say time longer than twine.

FALLING APART

"What the hell going on in here?" Ma shouted. "Get yuh so and so from out meh place." As I turned around to face Ma I could feel the disgust and coldness in her eyes, but when I turned around again Rajin was nowhere to be found. It was as if he was never there. I never thought of Rajin as a coward. I always thought of him as a strong, brave man who feared no one, not even Ma. He seemed to command the respect of all the young men in the village. The truth of the matter was that he ran behind the shed around the outhouse, through the cane field, and disappeared into thin air.

"And you, doh go so fast. Wait till yuh father and bredda come home this evening.

Yuh go dead for sure," Ma screamed. "This is how I raised yuh, yuh little wretch." These words rang out a thousand times in my head like the old rusty bell hanging outside the Roman Catholic church on the hill. I died a million deaths just contemplating the consequences. All the girls in the village around my age had boyfriends. They were kissing, fondling, and having intercourse, so what was the big deal. Every girl in the tiny village of Basterhall was engaging in some pleasure-seeking activity—unknown to their parents, of course. What was the big deal, I tried to comfort myself, playing it over and over in my disturbed, overstimulated mind. I knew being the only girl among five boys that my parents had great plans for me, so I was disappointed. I was more disappointed that I had disappointed them than kissing Rajin. I knew then that I had to take drastic action if I wanted to remain alive. With a half thought-out plan in my head, I dashed into the house and up the shaky, creaking wooden stairs.

The marigolds perfumed the atmosphere with an overpowering odor that caused everyone to rush to the shed in a panic. We always played outside late on weekends. All the girls and boys from the surrounding houses gathered on Friday and Saturday evenings. There was no other form of entertainment for us except the occasional village wedding or wake, so we looked forward to those meetings. It was one of those normal Friday evening gatherings that sent the peaceful village of Basterhall into an uproar. The cloudless sky suddenly turned a whitish peach. The huge golden ball of light sank slowly beneath the motionless horizon, leaving streaks of reddish-orange behind like an animal wounded and seeking assistance. As if the insects and animals understood, not a sound could be heard. Stillness choked me.

Rajin and I always met behind the shed for an evening smooch; at least, that was all he could offer me. But it felt like a hundred roses, a thousand hugs, and a million kisses. As his rough hands caressed my thick, long, oily ponytail, I wrapped my shiny dark arms around his sweaty back. The coconut oil glistened on his muscular body, making him all the more desirable. We held on to each other as if it were the last time we would be seeing each other. My father and brothers were never at home at that time during the weekends, and my mother would usually be busy finishing the evening meal. The *talkarie* would be cooked earlier; however, she would be making the *roti* because my father liked his *sada roti* hot. The smell of roasting *baigan* filled the dirt track so everyone knew that hot *sada roti* and *baigan choka* was the meal for the evening. It was safe to indulge in some mild excitement. I made sure of it. I checked their whereabouts several times before Rajin and I made this our routine. Of course, I also had my lookouts. However, Reeka and Kumarie were indulging in their own wild excitement that they failed to notice Ma coming behind the shed to pick up the *kuchela* and lime pepper sauce that she had put out to sun earlier.

Rajin was indeed the village catch. He was tall, muscularly endowed, and rugged looking. Some serious, rough masculinity wrapped up in sophistication. As if the gods had taken extra time to construct this specimen. Whenever he was near my heart tingled like a million butterflies fluttering around a bunch of *ixora* trying to extract nectar. He had "ah sweet mouth," as the old people used to say. This was a new feeling to me but a nice one. I grew up knowing Rajin. I had no recollection of my first encounter with him. It was as if I'd always known him.

My mother was the specimen of a goddess in my eyes. She was unusually tall for a woman, fair, with thick long jet-black hair. Her grayish-brown eyes lit up her whole face as she smiled. However, those same eyes pierced, sliced, minced, chopped, and whipped anybody to chutney if they angered her. Her small straight nose complemented her height. I always wondered what she saw in my father. His stomach protruded from his dark masculine body, and his thick shiny black hair always smelled of fresh coconut oil. His crooked teeth were stained yellow from years of being a slave to tobacco. My recollection of my father was that he was either at work on the sugarcane estate or rocking in the hammock eating something or smoking.

I ran all the way down the hill through the cane field. As hard as I tried, I was unable to hold back the tears. They flowed freely as a bankless river. I did not want to end up like my aunt Tara who was excommunicated from her family and familiar space. I knew that the perfect family had fallen apart and that would be the last time I would ever see the goddess again. My actions, even though driven by ear, was incomprehensible in the eyes of the villagers. I ran through the darkness yet forging a path of light as I trampled the shrubs and young cane stalks.

My intention was much like a fairy tale: to meet my handsome prince, run away, and live happily ever after. Little did I know that Rajin had plans of his own that did not include me. His warm hugs and passionate kisses convinced me that we shared the same sentiments.

I could hear the uproar and see the glowing of the flambeaux in the distance, and I knew they were looking for me. I slid my tiny frame into the drain and pulled the dry coconut branches over me. I held my breath as some of the villagers passed over me. It was an uneasy night for me in the coconut field as my physical body ached with pain from the harsh ground and the coconut roots as my mind wandered the globe. Fear consumed me whole at the thought of what would happen to me if my father and brothers found me. I'd barely shut my eyes when I heard the dogs barking and cocks crowing. I knew it was morning, so I cautiously crawled out of my hiding place. Suddenly I noticed Rajin's cousin, Sanjay, taking the cows out to graze. Sanjay was tall and lanky but handsome. He was a pleasant person with a good soul. I watched him lift the heavy mallet and bring it down onto the rusty iron crowbar with relentless force, trying to bury it into the hard, dry earth. Each blow harder than the previous one, as if he was impatient and just wanted to get this task over with. I motioned to him to quietly come to where I was hiding.

"Gyul, everybody looking for you," he exclaimed in a shocked voice.

"Is Rajin looking for me too?" I anxiously questioned.

"Ah tell you everybody," he responded impatiently.

"I want you to give Rajin a message for me. Tell him ah want to see him, tell him to meet me at Long Chinese grocery in Balmain at ten o'clock," I instructed.

His bright eyes glowed even brighter and he had a befuddled look on his face. "What? You know what you doing? You crazy. Gyul, just go back home and take yuh licks," was his response.

"Yuh know I char do that. I really love Rajin and I know he cares about me too. I know that you really care about Rajin's happiness as well."

Sanjay is not only Rajin's cousin but also his best friend. They were inseparable; they did everything together, so I was confident that Rajin would get the message with the same urgency that it was given. This would be the ideal time as the men would be at work in the cane field or the garden, the women would be busy preparing lunch, and the children would be playing, I reasoned to myself. The wait was an eternity. Ten a.m. felt like 10:00 p.m. I was confident that Sanjay would not disappoint me and that Rajin would come even if it was late. My stomach growled, not with hunger but fear and uncertainty. What was going to happen to my mother? Will she be able to live without me? And how will she manage? Would my father be able to forgive me? Would my brothers ever accept me as their sister again? What would the villagers think? What were Kumarie and Reeka doing at this time? How would this all end? Would Rajin and I have a big three-day traditional wedding? Sweat ran down my spine as fear made its way up. My knees became gelatinous and could hold me up no longer. I sat at the edge of the drain under the banana three trying to conceal myself yet allowing some visibility. The once clear sky became overcast and suddenly bullets of raindrops pelted from the sky. There was nowhere to go without being seen, so I sat still and allowed the heavy shower to wash over my polka-dot A-line dress. As the rain came down the dirt from the unpaved road traveled up my slender legs, leaving my rubber slippers muddy and my legs stockinglike.

I could hear the pulsating rhythm of the *tassa* as I joyfully and slowly made my way to the brightly decorated wedding marrow on the *Maticoor* night in my beautiful yellow organza sari. My thoughts were interrupted by Rajin's arrival. I was overwhelmed with ecstasy. My new life was about to begin. Rajin and I would finally be able to be together. This was all I ever wanted, his unconditional love and acceptance.

"Mala, I have to tell you something," he stuttered.

"What is it?" I excitedly questioned.

"My parents have arranged a marriage for me with a girl name Devica from Cumoto," he reluctantly said in a low tone and with a nonchalant look. "Everything is set already," he continued. His face was expressionless. The perfect son just following his parents' instructions. Ten thousand volts of electric current coursed through my skinny body. It must have fried my brain because I could not think. I was numb, I was speechless. I was too ashamed to go back home and too hurt to cry and too angry to lick down Rajin. I ran and could not stop. I cried and could not stop. Hundreds of thoughts raced through my disoriented mind. Who? When? What? Why? How?

There was only one place I could go. There was only one person I could turn to, my estranged aunt Tara from Cedros. Tara is my mother's youngest sister who was disowned by her parents and the rest of the family when she got pregnant out of wedlock. That was the last they head of Tara. However, I secretly kept in contact with her. I would walk a mile and a half to the post office under Mr. Pooran's house to mail and receive letters from her when I went to drop off fresh homemade ghee to Mr. Samlal at the shop.

As the sun started to dip behind the horizon to hide for the night, I decided to do the same. As the old cream Hillman Hunter drove off, I could not help but think how I had disappointed the goddess and the rest. But there was no turning back now. A feeling of ambivalence filled my soul. A new life in a new path awaited me.

The Scent of the Wild Orchid

It perfumed the air. It was the last of the purple blossoms. Not until next December will we experience the royal petals dancing over the wrought-iron fence. It was my favorite. I could spend hours just staring at the rich color and the thick, velvety texture. The scent was durable and unusual. It drew me in and kept me enrapt. Paula walked into the den holding out one hand and waving the other. I could sense an uneasiness in the air and smell that trouble was our neighbor. "Just look at this," she shouted. I moved close to the window to get away from her and to enjoy the last spray of nature's treasure. I was in no mood for conflict. I simply wanted to enjoy the view of the garden but in the comfort and shade. I loved to spend time with myself and my flowers. My mother's garden became my world. It was my escape from the never-ending familiar conflict that seemed to follow us no matter the distance. Marriage or geography was no match for this spirit. It has its roots deep, so it spread its branches wide and far. Paula had this habit of courting trouble and inviting conflict. She was the king of drama queens. I knew what she was about to say had trouble embossed on it.

Paula was referring to our mother's new will. She was furious. "How could she do this? Does Jason know about this? Do you know anything about this? What is really going on, who is advising her?" she blurted out with a litany of expletives. Mama had been ill for some time and was putting her house in order. She ordered the repainting and redesigning of the bungalow and an overhaul of the garden. She demanded that all the orchids be hung on the eastern side of the greenhouse, which stood next to the living and dining area, and the lilies be placed on the northern side. While all the other plants would be placed at designated spots. My mother's garden was breathtaking. The colors, the arrangement, the smells, all came together to create an enchanted space. The garden had been her passion and her lover after our father divorced her. She also rewrote her will, removing Paula and Jason completely while leaving me as the sole inheritor of our beautiful family mansion, inclusive of the vehicles, investments, money, and her treasured garden. Mother was a shrewd businesswoman with lots of investments. She'd lived a quiet life after my father left, choosing to focus on her work and her flowers.

"When you like an orchid you pick it, but when you love an orchid you water it," she would often say, quoting an old saying by Buddha. Her investments brought her amazing yields, so the monies were reinvested or went into travels or her garden. Her shoulder-length salt-and-pepper curly hair gave her a much thicker appearance. Her tiny gray eyes would smile back together with her thin pursed lips. She was a well-known virtuous woman in the community and business world and was admired by all, but my father's womanizing was also recognizable to these same people. We wanted for nothing. We had all the trappings and luxuries of life but my father's floundering around made us very indigent. I felt like we had nothing and needed everything.

After my father left and the property had to be settled, there was a squabble for the family's estate. Paula, being the eldest, thought that she was entitled to the major share, and also as her husband was the manager of one of our companies. Jason, being the only son, felt just as entitled. I, being the last, felt pressured. I wanted nothing but some peace and my family back together. This proved impossible. I had to run away from the grab for wealth while our parents were still alive and in their right minds. So I moved to one of the smaller Caribbean islands, started my very own flower shop business, and found love with a rugged horticulturist. While I worked with many beautiful flora, the wild orchids were my favorite. They reminded me of home and my mother. I made many trips back to spend time with my mother. When I accidentally found out that she was terminally ill, I made the difficult decision of closing my business indefinitely and moving back home to be close to her.

Our time was beautiful. We would go to bed singing, walk in the rain, sip coffee in the garden, bake black cake, redecorate in the middle of the day, and eat mangoes late in the night, have popcorn for breakfast. It was like old times again. She began living while she was dying. I watch her live and die daily with pride and sorrow.

"What do you think about some sapodillas?" Mama would suggest, giggling at ten in the night.

"Sounds perfect," I would say comfortingly. I was treated with ambivalence by the others. They were happy that I was taking care of Mama but they wanted to know when I was going back to my new home. I loved every minute of it, and I knew she loved it too. We enjoyed the tropical sunshine.

As I got the news my knees buckled under me and I collapsed on the sofa. The floodgates were open and there was no limit to its contents. Thoughts fluttered constantly, many unanswered questions raised their heads no matter how many time I silenced them. My stomach sank to the lowest part of my anatomy. It felt twisted and warped, like my entire being was one tiny ball. My life was reduced to memories only. I was now an orphan. Just two short years ago I was fatherless, now I am motherless. I could not bring myself to the place to even begin to process the next steps. It was a disgusting feeling. I felt like garbage left by the road for days, refused by those who were supposed to dispose of it. A dark and horrible place to be. How could one ever get out of this hole in the dark earth. Restriction of all my major organs was beginning.

As the days turned into weeks, my sadness turned into depression. My mourning spiraled out of control, my grouse was with every human being. I spent my days in bed with Blue as my only companion. The thick drapes were always pulled tight, hiding every glimmer of light. Darkness was my inner and outer companion. The gastric juices played games with my stomach and esophagus. I felt a terrible burning from my throat to my stomach that was resistant to antacids. Tablets to put me to sleep and tablets to calm my mind and tablets to assist with digestion and tablets to go to the washroom and tablets for everything.

My nostrils burned with the vanilla-like fragrance of the wild orchid. It made me nauseous. I could feel the bile rising in my throat. I hated the garden. The colors disturbed me, the smell sickened me to my stomach. When the fragrance wafted into the house on those windy days, it made me puke.

Suddenly it all came together. I was sleeping all day, I was moody, I was upset, and odors of things that I once enjoyed, like the wild orchid, made me nauseous. My depression turned into elation. I felt my mother move inside me and I was confident that all three of us would be okay.

WINNING SMILE

I presented my winning ticket, collected my money, and walked away smiling. Six, nine, two, one, and zero. I needed just a little bit of good luck, so I grabbed the lucky seed and rubbed it against my sweaty palms. Then I walked to the glass window, pushed my five-dollar bill, collected my receipt, and walked away. It was Tuesday evening and it was raining cats and dogs. The sky was gray and dull and the wind howled. The few bits of greenery amid the busy shopping area danced rhythmically. The bustle was on. Cars were tooting their horns, loudly inquiring of pedestrians if they needed transportation. People were everywhere, in the stores, outside the stores, on the pavement, on the road. Vendors were busy, the noise was deafening. Some were trying to cover their goods, while some were running for shelter; but still, others were trying to bargain off their produce for a reduced price.

I was now drenched in the cold rain and my teeth clattered. The constant droplets of rain impaired my vision. Cold began running down my nose and face, becoming one with the rain. I wasn't sure if the odd taste in my mouth was my own body fluid or nature's. My tennis shoes squelched in the puddles on the road as the pavements were occupied on both sides of the road. I pushed past the busy crowd and made my way to the taxi stand. There was a crowd at the taxi stand and not a single taxi in sight. Cold and hungry, I decided to get a cup of coffee from a nearby café. A beautiful young lady with a pleasant tone smiled as she handed me the steaming cup. "Here you go, sir," she said, flipping her hair to the other side. I accepted the cup, smiled back, and said, "Thank you. And what is the lucky number today?" Her bright huge eyes lit up like two rare gems before she blurted out some numbers. I hurriedly scribbled them on the back of my coffee receipt and headed out the door. I slowly walked back to the taxi stand but not before stopping at the corner shop to play the numbers that my mystery coffee lady gave me. I grabbed the lucky soiled bill and called out the numbers. "Six, nine, two, one, and zero," I said to the old bald man behind the counter. Little did I know that I was calling out the winning numbers.

It was almost an hour and a half before I was able to get a taxi. The drive seemed longer than usual. I just wanted to have a bath, have some dinner, and jump into my comfortable king-sized bed. My bed seemed softer and cozier than usual. It's funny how you appreciate the simple things in life when you are experiencing a bad patch, I thought to myself. I was scarcely finished praying when I dozed off. I must have fallen into a deep sleep because I did not hear the alarm.

I dreamt that I had won the lottery jackpot. I was beyond elated. I thought of all the things I wanted to buy but could not afford to. I ran into Premier variety store and started emptying it. I thought of my mom. She needed a house, my dad needed surgery, my brothers and sisters. I couldn't believe that simple me who had never won anything before, not even a school raffle, had won the jackpot. I had to get used to the idea that I could now buy anything, that I had lots of money. Suddenly I became scared, and beads of perspiration started to make their way down my back and into my trousers and above my lips.

I was sweating profusely when I jumped out of my sleep. I was super late for work. I was now confused. I felt disoriented, but luckily all bad things come to an end as well. At the end of a long, grueling day with a nagging supervisor and a desk full of filing to complete, I decided to end the day with a beautiful smile, good conversation if I was lucky, and of course, a cup of freshly brewed coffee. To my disbelief, the café was closed. I was bothered but made nothing of it. I chalked it up to a streak of bad luck, so I joined the waiting crowd to get home. Two beers and some roast pork was how I ended that long day. When you live alone, beer can quickly become a constant companion and fast food a confidant. Even with my two best buddies my coffee lady never left my mind.

Everyone sat anxiously at the bar listening and looking intently at the black and white screen. Wilsons was the ideal watering hole. The ambience was perfect, the service was topnotch, and the employees were attractive. The dim lights and the low music created a *tabanca* space. I was not too into the results, so I sat sipping on my stale beer, looking at the television but my mind on the coffee girl. I went back there in the evening but she was nowhere to be found. The little café was closed. What was odd was that I'd never gone into that café before even though I have waited for a taxi a thousand times at that same spot. I asked around but no one seemed to remember her. Something that particular day drew me into that café. Maybe it was the bad weather or the unpleasant day I was having.

"Are you having another one, sir?" the shapely Hispanic bartender whispered as she smiled in an inviting way.

"Maybe one more for the road," I smiled back in an "accepting the invitation" way. I could not believe my ears. The numbers I had on my slip were the numbers on the screen, in the exact order. I was numb. I said nothing to no one. I was afraid to even look at anyone lest my facial expression gave it away. I did not know how to react. I kept looking at my ticket and the screen. I asked a fat guy close by to repeat the numbers to me just to ensure that I had seen and heard correctly. I slowly tucked my winning ticket back into my battered wallet, tried to look disappointed and miserable, and strolled out of Wilsons for the last time.

My time and money were now elastic. I now had a lot, and neither one seemed to run out. I had quit my dull, boring job. Good days were many; love was everywhere, but I could not find my coffee lady. No one knew her or anything about her. She was an angel serving coffee. I could not get her brown eyes out of my mind, the way she smiled and whispered the numbers to me. I felt like I knew her from another life.